NEW EDITION

Wide Range Readers

BLUE BOOK 4

Fred J. Schonell
Phyllis Flowerdew

D0816207

Oliver & Boyd

Illustrated by John Harrold, Carol Holmes,
Peter Mousedale, R. A. Sherrington,
Michael Strand and Pat Tourret

Oliver & Boyd
Pearson Education Limited
Edinburgh Gate
Harlow
Essex CM20 2JE

An Imprint of Longman Group UK Ltd

First published 1949
Second edition 1965
Third edition 1976
Fourth edition 1985
Sixteenth impression 2000

ISBN 0 05 003746 3

Set in 14/20 pt 'Monophoto' Plantin
Printed in Singapore (KKP)
SWT/10

The publisher's policy is to use paper manufactured from
sustainable forests.

Preface

The Wide Range Readers are planned to provide graded reading practice for junior school children. Because children of 7–11 have a wide range of reading needs and attainments, there are three parallel series—Blue, Green and Red books —to provide plenty of material to suit the interests and reading ages of every child.

Books 1–4 are graded by half yearly reading ages, for use by appropriate groups within a class. Book 1 should provide an easy read for children with a reading age of about 7–7½. Children with reading ages below 7 are recommended to use the Wide Range Starters.

The controlled vocabulary of the series makes the books suitable for the following reading ages:

6½–7	**Starter Books**—Blue, Green and Red
7–7½	**Book 1**—Blue, Green and Red
7½–8	**Book 2**—Blue, Green and Red
8–8½	**Book 3**—Blue, Green and Red
8½–9	**Book 4**—Blue, Green and Red
9+	**Book 5**—Blue, Green and Red
10+	**Book 6**—Blue, Green and Red
11+	**Book 7**—Red only
12+	**Book 8**—Red only

Contents

The Missing Boat

In a shabby wooden hut, almost touching the ripples of the river, lived Old Mac. He had a brown, wrinkled face and a grey, curling beard. Everyone called him Old Mac, and if he had any other name, it had long ago been forgotten. He made his living by letting out rowing boats to people who wanted them for an hour or two, for a morning or even for a whole day.

He had twelve boats, which he kept tied to a little wooden platform at the water's edge.

In the winter when the wind was cold, and the grass on the hill was white with frost, he stored the boats in the hut, and went away to stay with his sister in the country.

In the spring he came back. He swept the hut, and made his bed on a wooden bunk at one end. He cleaned his saucepan and frying pan, and set them out on his oil cooking stove. He dusted his table and his two chairs. He pushed the boats out on the sand and painted them—some green, some blue, some brown—and left them to dry in the sun.

In the summer he was always busy, for people came nearly every day to hire boats.

Some rowed their families up the river for picnics among the rushes. Some rowed them down the river, and stayed fishing all day in the place where the river met the sea.

Every day Old Mac untied the ropes, waded into the water and pushed the boats off from the shore. He smiled at the people and always said,

"This is a fine little boat."

One night he was asleep in his hut. The river shone like silver, and the sand gleamed damp and bright beneath the moon. Everything was still, except for the gentle swaying of the rowing boats tied to the little wooden platform.

The moon peeped in at the open door and shone on Old Mac's face, but it didn't wake him. There were footsteps on the sand outside, but they didn't wake him.

So he didn't see someone small go creep, creeping down to the little wooden platform, and step into one of his boats. He didn't hear the oars dip, dipping in the water. He didn't know that someone was taking Blue Bird, his lightest and newest boat, down the river to the sea.

When Old Mac awoke in the morning, the river was shining in the sun, and the rowing boats were still swaying gently on the ripples. Proudly Old Mac looked at them, all so smart and bright and clean. But surely Blue Bird was in a different place! Last night he had left her on that side of the platform, and now she was on this side. It was very strange. He rubbed his eyes and stared.

"Perhaps I made a mistake," he said to himself at last. "Perhaps I did leave her on this

side after all." Just then someone came to ask for a boat, and Old Mac forgot about Blue Bird.

The next night the same thing happened again. As he slept, someone small came creep, creeping down the sand, stepped into the blue boat, dipped the oars in the silver water and glided down the river to the sea. In the morning when Old Mac looked at the rowing boats, he thought,

"That's strange. Blue Bird's cushion is on the middle seat, and I know I left it at the back last night." He was very puzzled.

The third night, instead of putting the oars neatly together under the seat, he placed them with the handles touching like a huge letter V.

"Now," he said, "if the oars are not in a V tomorrow, I'll know for certain that someone is taking Blue Bird out at night."

Next morning, of course, the oars were not in a V. They were placed neatly together at the bottom of the boat.

"Now I'm sure," said Old Mac.

For many nights he tried to keep awake to watch for the thief, but he was old and tired, and always, sooner or later, he fell asleep. Every morning when he looked at Blue Bird he knew someone had taken her out at night. Sometimes she was in the wrong place. Sometimes her oars were moved or her cushion was out of place. Sometimes there were splashes on her floor, and drips on her blue paint.

"I wish I knew who took her," thought Old Mac angrily. "I wish I knew."

One day, as he sat at the door smoking his

pipe in the sun, he had a sudden idea.

"Of course," he said slowly. "It must be the fairy folk! Perhaps they need a boat to take them to the island up the river. Perhaps they hold their midnight dances there." He chuckled to himself to think that they used one of *his* boats—sturdy little Blue Bird. Several times during the day he wrinkled up his brown face in a smile, and murmured,

"It's the fairies. Of course!"

That night, before he went to bed, he put food for them in Blue Bird. He put a rosy apple and a plate of bread and jam cut in very small pieces.

In the morning when he found the plate was empty, he was as pleased as could be. He hummed a merry tune as he waded in and out of the water, pushing the rowing boats away from the shore.

After that, whenever he walked to the village to do his shopping, he bought something extra for the little people's supper—apples or chocolate biscuits, or raspberry tarts. Every night he left something on a plate in Blue Bird. Every morning he found the food gone, the cushion out of place, the oars moved, and sometimes he found a fresh fish on the plate, for his breakfast.

Early one morning, while it was still dark, a storm arose. The waves from the sea came sweeping into the river. The river splashed and tossed upon the sand. The rowing boats were shaken and knocked together so much that the noise awoke Old Mac. He listened to the howling wind and the tossing water and the clattering boats.

"The paint will be spoilt," he thought. He put on his raincoat and went out into the darkness. One by one he pulled the boats up on the shore, out of reach of the waves. Blue Bird was not there.

"Poor little people," he said aloud. "It's a bad night for you to be out." He went back to bed.

When next he awoke, it was time for breakfast. The storm had passed, but the wind was still high. Old Mac looked at the rowing boats lying on the sand. Blue Bird had not returned.

"I hope she's safe," he murmured. "She's my very best boat. I shouldn't like to lose her."

No one came to hire boats that day. No one even passed the hut. The wind was too strong, and the waves were high.

Evening came, and still Blue Bird didn't return. Old Mac was worried. Perhaps she had been left somewhere, and she had drifted away on the tide. Perhaps she had been stolen, or had floated out to sea. Perhaps she had been thrown against the rocks and smashed to pieces. He felt most unhappy.

In bed, he lay awake a long time, listening and waiting, listening and waiting. The wind dropped. The night was calm and beautiful. Beneath the moon, the sand gleamed damp and bright. The river shone like silver. Old Mac fell asleep.

As soon as the sun arose next morning he went to the door to look out and see if Blue Bird had been brought back.

Yes! There tied to the wooden platform she lay, rocking gently up and down on the ripples. Her paint was badly scratched. She looked battered and worn.

Oh, how glad he was to see her! Quickly he dressed and hurried down the little wooden platform.

He stopped. He heard something—a deep, tired sigh. There was someone in Blue Bird! Was it one of the fairy folk?

Quietly he leaned over and looked inside. It

14

was *not* a fairy. It was a boy, fast asleep. His clothes were ragged and his feet were bare. His brown hair was rough and untidy.

"So it's you!" shouted Old Mac angrily. "It wasn't the fairies at all! It's you who's been stealing my boat all the summer. And look how battered she is now! Look at her!"

At once the boy awoke, jumped up on to the platform, and tried to run away, but Old Mac caught hold of his arm. The boy was so thin and small, and his wide brown eyes looked so frightened, that Old Mac was sorry he had spoken roughly.

"Were you out in the storm?" he asked more kindly.

"Yes," whispered the boy.

"All alone?"

"Yes."

"It's a big boat for a youngster like you to manage. Did you drift into the rocks?"

"Yes."

"You're tired, I guess."

"Yes."

"And hungry too?"

"Yes."

"Come into my hut," said Old Mac, "and I'll cook some breakfast for you. We can talk afterwards. Just tell me your name so I know what to call you."

"Patrick."

Old Mac led him into the hut, and pointed to a chair beside the wooden table. Patrick sat down. He watched Old Mac boiling water, frying bacon, and cutting bread. He watched everything he did, but he said not a word. Old Mac knew by the look in his wide brown eyes, that he hadn't seen or smelled or tasted such a fine meal for a very long time.

When he put a cup of tea and the breakfast in front of him, Patrick stared as if he were afraid to touch it. Then he gobbled it down so fast that Old Mac could hardly believe his eyes.

Soon, when they had both finished, Old Mac

said sternly,

"Now, young Patrick, I want to know why you've been stealing my boat every night this summer."

"Oh, not stealing," said Patrick quickly, "borrowing."

"Borrowing without asking is stealing. Where have you been with it?"

"Where the river meets the sea."

"What for?"

"To fish."

"And why did you have to take Blue Bird, my best and newest boat?"

"It was easier for me because it was the lightest of your boats."

"I see," said Old Mac gravely.

"Oh, please don't be angry with me," said Patrick, suddenly beginning to talk very fast. "I know I shouldn't have taken your boat—but you see, I've been fishing at night, and selling the fish in the daytime. I needed money to buy food, and to save up for the winter. It's such a good place to fish, where the river meets the sea.

"When I was caught in the storm, I couldn't manage the boat, and I was nearly wrecked on the rocks. I wasn't able to get back until late the next morning, so I landed further down on the other side of the river, so you wouldn't see me. Last night I brought Blue Bird back early, because I was so tired, and there were no fish. I rested for a while, but I didn't mean to sleep so long.

"The food you put in the boat every night was meant for the fairy folk, wasn't it? I ate it of course."

He stopped talking as suddenly as he had started, and then added, "I'm sorry."

"You're a brave boy," said Old Mac. "Have you a mother and father?"

"No."

"No one to look after you at all?"

"No," said Patrick unhappily.

Old Mac stroked his grey, curling beard, and stared at the boy for a long time without saying anything. Then he said slowly,

"You shouldn't borrow, you know, without asking."

"It wasn't really borrowing," murmured Patrick.

"Not borrowing? Not stealing? What was it then?"

"It was pretending," said Patrick. "I pretended you were my grandfather, and you sent me fishing every night. I pretended you stood at the hut door and said, 'You'll find your supper in the boat. Goodnight, my boy.' Always as I dipped in the oars and rowed away, I whispered, 'Goodnight, Grandfather,' to you."

"Oh, you did, did you?"

"Yes."

"Would you like it to be like that?"

"Oh, yes." For the first time that day Patrick smiled. "I could help you a lot," he said. "I could paint the boats for you, and help you push them out when people hired them. I

could do your shopping for you, and—"

"And come with me in the winter, to stay with my sister in the country?"

"Oh, yes—please."

Old Mac looked round the hut.

"I think I've enough wood to make you a bed in here," he said. "Help me push the boats into the water, and then we can start on it."

Eagerly Patrick ran across the sand and pushed the boats out, so that Old Mac could tie them to the little wooden platform. They rocked gently up and down on the ripples. The river shone like silver. The sand gleamed damp and bright in the morning sunshine.

"Patrick!" called Old Mac, wrinkling up his brown face in a smile. "I think you'd better pull Blue Bird up on the shore, so that I can see whether the rocks have damaged her. Then we'll get on with that bed of yours."

Patrick stood up, and pushed back his untidy brown hair.

"Yes, Grandfather," he said.

The Tale the Geese Tell

Have you ever noticed how geese strut along
with their heads in the air, as if they are very
proud of themselves? Perhaps they do it because
they are made that way, but it may be because
they remember the story their mothers told
them when they were young. It is a true story
of something that happened hundreds and
hundreds of years ago.

Once long ago, some geese lived in a garden
in the city of Rome. They were very contented,
for they had plenty to eat and nothing to do
except to sit in the sunshine and chatter to each
other. Sometimes wild geese came that way, and
told them the latest news. Then the wild geese
flew away again, their long necks stretched out,
and their wings flapping up and down through
the blue sky.

The geese in the garden began to think that
the sky would always be blue, that there would
always be plenty to eat, and that life would

always be peaceful and pleasant.

But one day everything changed. The air was filled with noise and shouts and cries. Grey smoke appeared like clouds all around, and the sky was red with the glowing of fires.

"What's happening?" the geese said to each other, and they cackled and hissed and were afraid because they didn't understand. Soon the wild geese flew overhead, in an anxious chattering crowd.

"Fly away while you can," they cried. "You're in danger. Fly away!"

The geese in the garden looked up at their friends in the smoky sky.

"What's happening?" they called. "What's happening?"

"There's a great battle," the wild geese replied. "The Gauls have come. They are fierce and warlike men. They're fighting the people of Rome. They're driving them from their homes. They're setting the city on fire. Fly away while you can!"

Through the choking clouds of smoke flew the wild geese, through the glowing red sky, into the distance and out of sight. The geese in the garden stood still.

"Shall we fly away?" they wondered.

"We've always been happy here," said one. "Perhaps the battle will soon be over. Perhaps the fierce Gauls will be driven from the city, and we'll be left in peace."

"Manlius hasn't gone away," said another, "for the door of his house is still open."

The geese turned their heads towards the

house where Manlius lived. They all knew him, for he was a friendly man, who often looked over the wall, and threw scraps to them.

"While Manlius stays, we will stay," decided the tallest of the geese, and so they stayed.

The battle went on for many days. Houses were burnt and people were driven away. But the garden where the geese lived, and the houses near by, were kept safe because they were on a high, rocky hill with steep sides that were hard to climb. Again and again the fierce Gauls tried to find a way up through the rocks and the bushes.

"There must be a secret way," they said. "We'll keep looking until we find it."

Meanwhile the people in the high, safe part of the city were getting short of food. They wondered where the rest of the Romans were hiding, and they wished they could send a message to them. Manlius was often hungry, and he hardly had any scraps to throw over the wall to the geese. The geese grew thin, but they didn't fly away.

"While Manlius stays, we will stay," they said.

All this time the rest of the Romans were sheltering in another town not far away.

"We must send a message to the people on the hill in Rome," they said, so a brave young soldier offered to take it.

One night he crept round the edge of the Gauls' camp, and they didn't hear him. He crept up the secret way through the bushes and the rocks. He climbed the steep hill, and came out among the houses on the top. How glad the

Romans were to see him, and to hear that their friends were safe.

In the morning the Gauls began once more to look for a way up the hill. Suddenly one of them saw a footprint. Then he noticed a tuft of grass bent over where someone had stepped upon it.

"A Roman has climbed up during the night!" he cried. They found more footprints, and so they discovered the way the soldier had gone— round the rocks and through the bushes, up to the very top of the hill.

"Tonight when it's dark," they said, "we'll creep up and surprise the Romans. We'll

attack them, and burn their houses. Then the city of Rome—all of it—will belong to us."

Night came. It was very dark, for the moon was hidden by clouds, and even the stars were asleep. It was very still, for there was no wind to rustle the grasses or sigh in the trees. In the safe part of Rome, high up on the top of the rocky hill, the people slept. Manlius slept in his house. The geese slept in their garden. Even the soldier who walked up and down to guard the city became sleepy.

"We're quite safe," he thought. "The Gauls will never find the way up the hill." He sat down to rest for a moment. His eyes closed and he fell asleep.

Up the hill, creeping, creeping through the silent night came the Gauls. Over the rocks and through the bushes they came, up, up, up in the darkness. So quietly they crept that no one heard them. The people in the city went on sleeping. Manlius in his house went on sleeping. Even the guard on duty went on sleeping. It seemed as though this would be the end of Rome.

But in the garden, the geese awoke. They heard creeping footsteps and the rustle of grass. They heard the fierce Gauls coming nearer and nearer to the top of the hill. In a moment the geese were up on their feet. They stretched their long necks. They hissed and cackled and hissed as loudly as they could, as if they knew that Rome was in danger.

The noise woke Manlius, and he leapt out of bed. Rushing out into the darkness, he saw the first Gaul reach the top of the hill. Manlius caught hold of him and pushed him back with all his might! Then he waited for the next, and as he waited he shouted, and awoke the Roman soldiers. Out of their houses they tumbled with their spears and shields. They rushed to the edge of the hill. They fought the Gauls as they appeared over the rocks and through the bushes. They pushed them back and drove them away.

So the city of Rome was saved by the cackling of the geese in the garden.

Have you ever noticed how geese strut along with their heads in the air, as if they are very proud of themselves? Perhaps they are. Perhaps they remember the story their mothers told them when they were young—the story about the geese who saved the city of Rome.

Help!

It was raining. The Gang were having to meet indoors for the second time that week.

"Move up, please," said Dawn. She was trying to push her way into a corner of the shed.

"Don't push like that," squeaked Angela. "I'll fall off this box!"

"Oh, stop arguing, you two," said Clarrie. "We'll have my Mum out here to see what's going on. You know we're not supposed to play in the shed."

Dawn looked round the tiny garden hut. She wriggled into a corner to sit on a flower-pot.

"Not much good anyway, is it?" she said. "Some Gang Hut."

"Better than the one you haven't got, then!" said Clarrie. Angela giggled.

"Let's get down to business," said Clarrie. "We were going to talk about what we should be doing for the Easter holidays."

"School holidays are boring!" said Dawn.

"We could do a pop concert," said Angela. The other two looked at her and shook their heads.

"I had this idea last night," said Clarrie.

"Oh, not again!" said Dawn. "I remember the idea you had at Christmas. My Dad was furious. He said a policeman's daughter shouldn't behave like that!"

"I was reading this book in bed," said Clarrie, ignoring her. "It was about Robin Hood. It told how he used to rob the rich people so that he could give things to the poor."

"We're not going to go out and rob people, are we?" said Dawn. "My Dad'll love that!"

"Idiot!" said Clarrie. "What we're going to do is go around doing good things for people who need help. But we won't tell them it's us. It'll be a surprise."

"You mean, my Mum might get up one morning and find that the kitchen's been re-decorated?" said Dawn. "Dad said he'd do it months ago, but he never did."

"Yes ... well, that kind of thing," said Clarrie.

"Sounds a bit daft to me," said Dawn. "But it could be fun. What'll we do first?"

"We could tidy up my Grandad's garden," said Angela. "He's always moaning about the weeds. If we go round this afternoon he'll be out at the bowling green."

"Good idea," said Clarrie. "He'll be really pleased to come back and find it's all done. We'll meet outside the house after lunch. And bring a fork or a trowel with you."

That afternoon, they waited until Angela's Grandad had gone and then crept round to his back garden.

"It looks as though he's done most of it himself," said Dawn. The flower-beds had been freshly dug.

"Except for that bit there," said Clarrie. "And all those funny weedy little plants."

They crawled along the damp, muddy flower-bed, digging out all the little green plants. Then they put them in the dustbin.

That night, as Angela's family were having tea, the telephone rang. Mum went to answer it, and talked for a long time.

"That was your Grandad," she said at last. "He's furious. Some little vandals got into his garden this afternoon and dug up all his cabbage plants. He'd just spent the morning putting them in, too."

Angela coughed into her teacup.

"It went down the wrong way," she said.

"You should be more careful, then," said

her Mum. "Just imagine. You never know what'll happen next. Mrs Jenks' house was broken into on Saturday and they took her silver teapot."

The Gang met in the park next morning.

"That wasn't a very good idea," said Dawn.

"Never mind," said Clarrie. "We'll do something better next time."

But the next idea was worse! They decided to decorate Dawn's kitchen.

"We can wait till Saturday," said Dawn. "Dad takes Mum to the supermarket. I'll tell her I'm coming round to your house, Clarrie. Then we can do the kitchen after they've gone."

"I don't know," said Clarrie.

"It's easy," said Dawn. "I've helped Dad do it before. All you do is pull off the old paper, paste the new stuff and stick it up. It only took him an afternoon to do my bedroom. And Mum's bought the new kitchen paper already."

"All right," said Clarrie. "If you're sure."

But it wasn't so easy. When they pulled off

the paper with the flowers on it there was
another one underneath.

"That's horrible!" said Clarrie. "All those

lettuces and tomatoes and green things. It looks as though there are caterpillars in there."

They started to pull off the lettuce paper and found a blue and white one underneath that.

They scraped and pulled. Some pieces of the paper came away easily. Other pieces stuck very firmly to the wall. It took hours, and before they were half-way round the kitchen Dawn's Mum and Dad came home.

"Oh dear, oh dear, oh dear!" said Dawn's Mum, sitting down hard on a kitchen chair. Dawn's Dad just stared. He looked as if he was going to explode.

"I don't think we should have done that," said Clarrie later.

"I don't know," said Dawn. "I don't think Mum minded too much. At least Dad will *have* to paper the kitchen now."

A few days later, the girls were wandering round the park, looking for something to do.

"We could pick up the litter," said Angela. "Nobody would mind us doing that."

"Good thinking," said Clarrie. They spent the rest of the afternoon picking up sweet papers and crisp bags and fishing wooden ice-lolly sticks out of the pond.

"You see those bushes over there," said Clarrie. "There's an old bag stuffed under them."

They crawled in under the high green bushes along the path and pulled out a plastic bag.

"Into the bin with it," said Clarrie, picking it up. Then she stopped and felt the bag. "I know what this is. Look!" She opened the bag and took out a little round silver teapot. The girls turned it over and stared at it. On a little panel on the side it said:

Annie Margaret Williams   Andrew David Jenks
10th June 1937

"Mrs Jenks' silver teapot!" they all said together.

Dawn's father returned the teapot to Mrs Jenks. She was delighted to have it back.

"It's got a few more dents now," she said. "But at least it's home again." Mr Jenks gave the girls a reward.

"Isn't it funny," said Dawn. "We set out to be like Robin Hood and we end up with the people giving *us* money."

"You know," said Clarrie looking at the pound notes. "I've just thought of something we could do during the summer holidays."

"Oh no!" said Dawn and Angela together.

Moira Miller

Why the Sea is Salt

Once upon a time there were two brothers, one poor and the other rich. The poor brother was walking home from his work one evening, carrying a piece of bacon, when suddenly he met an old woodcutter. He thought it strange that he hadn't noticed him till that moment, and he thought it strange that he had heard no footsteps.

"Good evening," said the poor brother.

"Good evening," replied the old woodcutter. He looked hopefully at the piece of bacon, and said,

"Please give me that bacon. I'm very hungry."

"I'm sorry," said the poor brother. "I can't give it away. If I do, my wife and I will have nothing to eat for our supper."

"Please give me the bacon," said the woodcutter again, "and I'll give you this little mill for grinding flour."

"I've nothing to grind into flour," replied

the poor brother.

"Ah!" said the old woodcutter. "This mill doesn't need anything. It grinds by itself. It grinds almost anything."

The poor brother waited a moment. Then he said,

"All right. I'll change with you."

He gave the bacon to the woodcutter, and the woodcutter gave him the little mill and showed him how to make it work.

When the poor brother reached home at last, his wife met him at the door, saying,

"What have you brought for supper? I'm so hungry."

"Wait and see," said the poor brother, and he put the mill on the table.

"What good is a mill to us?" asked his wife. "We've nothing to grind into flour."

But the poor brother made the mill grind out a tablecloth, then meat, then bread and butter, then apples and grapes, until the table was filled with everything they needed. His wife stared in surprise.

"What a wonderful mill," she said. "Where did you get it?" But the poor brother wouldn't tell her.

Three days later he gave a great feast and asked his rich brother to come.

"This is strange," said the rich brother. "Usually you're so poor that you haven't enough food for yourself to eat. Now you give a great feast as if you're a king. Where did you get all this?"

At first the poor brother wouldn't tell him. But later in the evening he showed him the mill, and made it grind all kinds of things.

"There!" he said. "This is where I get my riches."

As soon as the rich brother saw the mill, he wanted it for himself. The poor brother refused to give it to him, but at last he said,

"All right. If you want it so badly, I'll let you have it for three hundred pieces of silver." So the rich brother counted out three hundred silver pieces, and the poor brother gave him the mill, but he didn't tell him how to work it. The rich brother felt very pleased and excited, and he carried the mill back to his farm.

Next morning the rich brother said to his wife,

"I'll stay and get the dinner ready today. You go into the field and toss the hay. I'll call you when it's time to come back."

When it was nearly dinner time, the rich brother said to himself,

"We'll have herrings and soup today." He turned the handle and said,

"Grind herrings and soup, and grind them fast."

At once the mill began to grind out herrings and soup. First it filled all the dishes. Then it filled all the tubs.

"That's enough!" cried the rich brother. He turned the handle of the mill to make it stop, but it didn't stop. He twisted and turned the handle again, but the mill went on grinding and grinding, herrings and soup, herrings and soup, herrings and soup. Soon the kitchen floor was covered with herrings and soup.

"Stop! Stop!" cried the rich brother, but though he twisted and turned the handle of the mill, he couldn't make it stop. On it went, grinding and grinding, herrings and soup, herrings and soup, herrings and soup.

The brother ran to the kitchen door, and then into the dining room. But the mill went on grinding until the dining room was filled with herrings and soup too, and the brother had to swim to reach the front door. It was

difficult to get hold of the latch, with all the soup and herrings swirling round him, but at last he managed it. He pushed open the front door and ran out. He hurried down the road, with a river of herrings and soup rushing and roaring like a waterfall just behind him.

Now all this time, his wife had been tossing hay in the field.

"My husband is a long time calling me in to dinner," she thought. "Perhaps he can't make the soup properly. I'd better go home and help him." She put down the hay fork, and walked slowly towards the house.

Before she had gone very far, what should she see but a dashing, splashing river of herrings and soup, and her husband running before it as fast as he could run!

"Take care you're not drowned in the soup!" he called, and away he went. He didn't stop running till he reached his poor brother's house.

"Please take back the mill," he begged.

"I don't want it back," said the poor brother.

"If it grinds much more," cried the rich brother, "the whole village will be swallowed up in herrings and soup."

"All right," said the poor brother. "Give me

three hundred more pieces of silver, and I'll take back the mill."

So the poor brother took the mill again, and stopped it grinding; and the river of herrings and soup dashed and splashed away and was seen no more.

Now that the poor brother had the mill again, he made it grind many more things for him. Soon he became rich enough to buy a large farm near the sea. His new farmhouse was bigger and better than the one in which his rich brother lived. Then he made the mill grind gold for him. It ground so much that he was able to cover the whole house with pieces of gold.

How the golden house gleamed in the sunlight! Sailors in their boats far across the sea could see it shining in the distance.

Soon everyone in the land had heard of the golden house and the wonderful mill; and people came from far and wide to see the marvellous sight.

One day a captain came over the sea in l...
ship. He saw the golden house shining in the
sun, and he knew that the wonderful mill was
inside it.

"I wish I had a mill like that," he said.
For year in, year out the captain had to sail
across the stormy seas and back again to bring
salt from other lands.

"If I had that mill," he thought, "I could
make it grind salt. Then I shouldn't have to
sail to other lands to fetch it." He made up his
mind that he would buy the mill, even if it cost
all the money he had saved. So he brought his
ship to shore, and he walked across the fields to
the golden house. He asked to see the wonderful
mill.

"Can it grind salt?" he asked.

"Of course!" said the brother. "It can grind
anything."

"Will you sell it to me?" asked the captain.

For a long while the answer was "No," but
the captain begged and begged so hard, that

in the end the brother said,

"All right. If you want it so badly, I will let you have it for a thousand silver pieces."

The captain paid the money, and took the mill. He left the house in a great hurry because he was afraid the man might change his mind, and so he forgot to ask how the mill worked. He ran across the fields to his ship, and he sailed far out to sea.

Then he put the mill on deck and said,

"Grind some salt, and grind it fast."

At once the mill began to grind salt. It filled the tubs and it filled the sacks.

"That's enough!" said the captain, and he turned the handle to make the mill stop. But it didn't stop. It went on and on, grinding more and more salt. Soon the whole deck was covered in salt, and the pile grew higher and higher like a white mountain.

"Stop! Stop!" cried the captain, and he twisted and turned the handle, but the mill went on and on, grinding more and more salt.

"If it grinds much more," thought the captain, "the salt will sink my ship." He was so afraid this would happen that he picked up the mill, held it high above his head and threw it far into the sea.

There to this very day lies the mill, at the bottom of the sea, grinding and grinding, salt, salt and yet more salt.

And that is why the sea is so salty.

Adapted

The Boys who made Aeroplanes

Not so long ago, if people had anything very difficult to do, they used to laugh and say,

"I might as well try to fly." That seemed the most impossible thing in the world, for no one had thought of aeroplanes.

At that time, there lived in America two little boys whose names were Wilbur and Orville Wright. One day their father came home and said,

"Here's a present for you," but he kept the present hidden behind his back.

"Please let's see," said Orville.

"What is it?" asked Wilbur.

"Guess," said Father.

"Sweets!" shouted Orville.

"A game!" cried Wilbur.

Father shook his head.

"Catch it," he said, and threw it towards them. But the present didn't fall into their open hands. It flew up to the ceiling, fluttered a moment, and then landed softly on the floor.

"It's like a bird!" exclaimed Orville in delight.

"It's a tiny flying machine!" cried Wilbur, and he ran to pick it up, to see how it worked. It was made of paper and thin strips of wood,

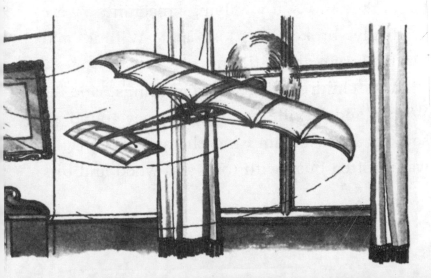

and it was wound up by twisting rubber bands. Wilbur sent it up to the ceiling again, and Orville laughed and tried to catch it as it fluttered down.

"Thank you, Father," they said. "It's a lovely present."

They played with it for a long while, and then tried to make one like it. Wilbur did most of the work because he was older, but Orville watched, and did what he could. When it was finished, it flew very well, up to the ceiling and down again.

"Now let's make a bigger one," said Orville, so they made one just a little bigger, and another just a little bigger still. Then, after a week or two, the tiny, toy, flying machines were gradually broken or lost and Wilbur and Orville forgot about them.

Most children like making things, and as Wilbur and Orville grew older, they found all sorts of ways of amusing themselves. Orville was so often busy with tools and wood and bits

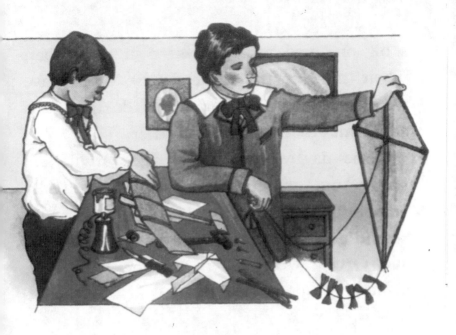

of iron, that his mother cleared out a room for him. Wilbur spent most of his time reading and writing, but he was always ready to help his brother, and between them they had some fine ideas.

They made kites to fly in the wind. They made a telegraph line between their house and the house of a friend. They borrowed some stuffed animals, and gave a grand circus show, with small birds and a great big bear. They played with a toy printing press, and then built a big one, and printed their own newspaper. Their mother and father must often have wondered what the pair would do next, and sometimes they said to each other,

"One day when Wilbur and Orville are grown up, they'll make something really wonderful."

And they were right. One day when Wilbur and Orville were grown up, they *did* make something wonderful!

★   ★   ★   ★   ★   ★

In France there lived a man who was making gliders. The brothers read about him.

"How nice it must be," said Orville, "to glide through the air from the side of a hill."

"Do you remember that toy flying machine we had when we were small?" asked Wilbur.

"Yes. I remember."

"Well, I don't see why it shouldn't be possible to make a big one—large enough to carry one person or even more."

Orville thought for a while, and then his

eyes gleamed with excitement and he said,
"Let's try."

That was the beginning of many years of hard work. The brothers read all the books about flying that they could find. They studied wings and wind and weather. They made drawings and plans, and tried out one idea after another. They built a glider and made it fly. Then they felt they were ready to build a flying machine—not just a glider with no power to send it along—but a real aeroplane with an engine, for a person to drive.

For months they worked hard, building the machine and the engine and measuring the wings. They found it hard to make the propellers, but they kept on trying, and at last the machine was finished.

"Now," said Wilbur, "we'll try it. Who will have the first turn?"

"Let's toss up," replied Orville. They tossed a coin.

"Heads!" cried Wilbur.

"Tails!" said Orville.

They looked anxiously as it fell. Each brother hoped so much that he would be the lucky one.

Heads! It was Wilbur! Excitedly he took his place in the flying machine. It rose into the air. It stayed up three and a half seconds, and then landed.

"Now it's my turn," said Orville. Up into the air he went, and down again.

"Twelve seconds!" said Wilbur.

Wilbur tried again, and stayed up nearly thirteen seconds. Orville tried. The machine was steadier this time and stayed in the air for fifteen seconds.

"One more try," he said. "Your turn, Wilbur." He got out to watch.

Once again Wilbur took his place in the machine, and rose into the air. Orville looked at his watch and counted the seconds. Ten, twenty, thirty, forty, fifty, fifty-nine. Fifty-nine seconds! Nearly a whole minute. The flying machine really worked! Wilbur and Orville

Wright were the first people in the world who had flown through the air. They had made the first petrol-driven flying machine—the first real aeroplane!

Even then there were people who didn't believe it.

"It's impossible!" they said. "If people were meant to fly, then babies would be born with wings. We'll never be able to travel through the air in a flying machine!" But they were wrong. As everyone now knows, aeroplanes had come to stay.

The Page Boy and the King

The servants of the King sat by the kitchen fire, and watched it blazing and crackling in the hearth.

"It's a bitter night," said the gardener, throwing another pine log on to the flames. "There'll be more snow before morning. You'll see."

"I'm glad I haven't to go out in it," remarked the Page Boy. He shivered at the very thought of the white world outside, and he pulled his stool a little nearer to the warmth. The cook started telling a story about the days when he was young. The Page Boy leaned against him, and was very comfortable. His cheeks grew pink, and he became more and more sleepy. He listened no longer to what the cook was saying, and a little later he didn't even hear his voice.

"Wake up! Wake up!" cried someone suddenly. The Page Boy rubbed his eyes. He must have been asleep.

"What's the matter?" he murmured.

"King Wenceslas wants you," said the gardener. "Run along. Don't keep him waiting."

"Oh, dear," wailed the Page Boy. "I was *so* comfortable."

He hurriedly smoothed his hair, and ran out of the kitchen.

He found the King sitting by a window. At the sound of the boy's footsteps, the King turned round and said,

"Here, Page, stand by me a moment."

The Page Boy went to the King's side, and looked out into the night. He saw snow lying in great heaps at the side of the path. He saw pine trees, white and sparkling in the moonlight.

"It looks beautiful, Sire," said the Page Boy, "but it's very cold. The gardener says it will snow again tonight." Even as he spoke, he noticed snowflakes beginning to fall again.

"Yes, it looks beautiful," agreed the King. "But that wasn't what I called you to see." He pointed to a man among the pine trees. "That poor old man," he said. "Who is he? And where does he live?"

"He lives quite a long way from here, Sire," replied the Page Boy. "He has an old hut at the foot of the mountain."

"Do you know where?"

"Oh, yes, Sire. It's right against the forest

fence, by Saint Agnes' fountain. I passed it once in the summer time."

The King gazed out and watched the old man, until he was lost to sight among the trees. Then still he sat at the window, saying nothing, and the Page Boy didn't know quite whether to stay or to go away. After a while he moved his feet and said,

"Is that all you want to know, Sire?"

"Page," said the King slowly. "You and I live in a strong castle, with great fires to keep us warm. We have thick clothes and good food. We don't know what it is to be really cold or hungry."

"No, Sire."

"Have you ever thought of the people who are poor—with rough little huts that let in the wind—with nothing much to eat, and not even enough sticks for the fire?"

"Sometimes, Sire."

"That poor old man we saw—he was hoping to find a branch broken down by the snow."

King Wenceslas paused a moment. Then he said, "Page, bring me meat and wine. Bring me pine logs. You and I will take a dinner to that old man tonight. Go to the kitchen and ask Cook to give you a bag of food, the best he can find."

"Yes, Sire," said the Page Boy. He said it rather sadly, for he had hoped to return to the blazing fire and sit there until bedtime. It would be cold out of doors—oh, so cold!

Soon everything was ready. King Wenceslas held a big bag of food under his cloak. The Page Boy carried the lantern and a bundle of pine logs. Out into the dark night they walked, past the great heaps of snow at the side of the path, and over the hill at the edge of the forest. The air was full of whirling snowflakes, and a bitter wind blew.

Faster and faster fell the snowflakes. Louder and louder moaned the wind. A cloud covered the moon, and only the swinging lantern glowed bravely in the darkness.

"We'll soon be there," said the King cheerfully. The Page Boy smiled up at him, but he felt most unhappy. The snowflakes stung his face. The pine logs under his arm kept slipping. His hand was almost too cold to hold the lantern, and his feet were simply freezing.

"Think what a lovely surprise these things will be for that poor old man," said the King as he plunged through the deep snow. "Why! I don't suppose he's ever had so much food in his life. And what a good fire he'll be able to have in his hut tonight!"

"Yes, Sire," murmured the Page Boy sadly. What a long, long way it seemed, and they weren't nearly there yet. And he was so cold, so cold. The pain in his feet and hands was almost

more than he could bear. He stumbled along
beside the King as well as he could. Then at last
he said,

"Sire, the night is darker now, and the wind
grows stronger. I can hardly walk—and I'm so
cold. I—I can't go on any longer."

King Wenceslas stopped, and took the
lantern. He held it up in the wind and the snow,
and in its light he saw the unhappy face of the
little Page Boy.

"We mustn't turn back now we've come
so far," he said kindly. "I'll carry the lantern,
so that you can keep your hands under your
cloak. We shan't be long now. You walk

behind me, and I'll protect you from the wind. I'll take shorter steps too. Then you can put your feet in my footprints, and perhaps you won't be so cold."

The Page Boy smiled a little.

"That's better," said King Wenceslas. "Be brave, my Page," and on he went.

The Page Boy walked behind the King, where the wind and the snowflakes could not blow so strongly in his face. Wherever the King stepped, he stepped, putting his feet in the King's footprints. It was like a game. The Page Boy felt happier, and began to get warmer. Even his cold, cold feet began to feel a little better. It was strange, but the footprints the King left seemed to be actually hot!

"How are you feeling now?" asked the King a little later.

"Oh, Sire, it's wonderful!" smiled the Page Boy. "I'm not cold at all. Your footprints are warm—hot like a fire."

The King laughed.

"Oh, no," he said. "It's not my footprints that are making you warm. It's your own brave heart."

The Page Boy was filled with happiness at the King's praise, and now just ahead, he saw Saint Agnes' fountain, and a little old hut. How surprised the poor old man would be when they knocked at his door, and gave him the bag of food and the bundle of pine logs.

How glad the Page Boy was that the King had asked *him* to go. It was a lovely idea! Strange how warm the King's footprints were. The Page Boy wondered about it. He gazed at the snow sparkling in the lantern light.

"I know," he thought to himself. "King Wenceslas is so good and kind, that even his footprints are warm."

But now there was no more time to wonder, for the King was knocking at the door, and inside the hut the old man was unfastening the latch.

Good King Wenceslas

Good King Wenceslas looked out
On the feast of Stephen,
When the snow lay round about,
Deep, and crisp, and even.

Brightly shone the moon that night,
Though the frost was cruel,
When a poor man came in sight,
Gath'ring winter fuel.

King: "Hither, page, and stand by me,
If thou know'st it, telling,
Yonder peasant, who is he?
Where and what his dwelling?"

Page: "Sire, he lives a good league hence,
              Underneath the mountain;
              Right against the forest fence,
              By Saint Agnes' fountain."

King: "Bring me flesh, and bring me wine,
              Bring me pine logs hither;
              Thou and I will see him dine,
              When we bear them thither."

              Page and monarch forth they went,
              Forth they went together;
              Through the rude wind's wild lament
              And the bitter weather.

Page: "Sire, the night is darker now,
              And the wind blows stronger;
              Fails my heart, I know not how,
              I can go no longer."

King : "Mark my footsteps, good my page;
Tread thou in them boldly:
Thou shalt find the winter rage
Freeze thy blood less coldly."

In his Master's steps he trod,
Where the snow lay dinted;
Heat was in the very sod
Which the saint had printed.

Therefore, Christian men, be sure,
Wealth, or rank possessing,
Ye who now will bless the poor,
Shall yourselves find blessing.

JOHN MASON NEALE

The Church that Crossed the Sea

Tom and Jimmy and Jean and Wendy lived in London. There was nowhere for them to play. There was not a garden, not a park, not a bit of waste land anywhere near. There were only grey streets and long lines of noisy traffic.

The street where they lived was just like all the other streets round about, except for one thing. In it was an old, old church. It was small and beautiful. It was left behind from another age. For hundreds of years it had been filled with music and voices, but now it was empty and silent. Its roof was tumbling in, and creeping plants had grown over the doors and windows, and locked them as firmly as any lock.

"I suppose the old church will be taken down one day," said the local people sometimes, "and someone will build a block of flats in its place."

Then one day it seemed as if they were right, for some builders arrived to do that very thing.

"I suppose they'll bash it down," sighed Tom.

"With a bulldozer," said Jimmy.

But the men didn't bash the church down. Nor did they use a bulldozer. They put up scaffolding, and they painted a number on every stone. Then they started to take the church down carefully, bit by bit, stone by stone.

On Saturdays and after school, the children stood round to watch. Tom and Jimmy and Jean and Wendy were joined by all the children in the street, and by other children from other streets.

"Why don't you bash it down?" Tom asked a workman one day.

"With a bulldozer?" added Jimmy.

"Oh no!" replied the workman. "It's too beautiful to destroy. It's going to be built up again somewhere else."

"Where?" asked the children.

"I'll tell you," said the workman. "This church is going right across the sea to America."

"Across the sea!" cried the children.

"Yes. They haven't any beautiful old churches like this in America. All these stones will be stacked up on a cargo ship and taken across the sea. Then the church will be built up again in America. Every stone will be put back in its right place. Every window will have new stained glass. It's a nice thought, isn't it?"

It *was* a nice thought, and for a few moments the children were silent.

"Won't it cost a lot of money to take it to America?" asked someone at last.

"Oh yes. It will. But the American man who is paying for it is very rich. He's an old man, called Mr Black. When he was a child, he used to live round here, and he used to go to this church on Sundays."

So the children ran home and told the news to their families. Everyone was glad that the church was going to have such a happy ending to its story.

Week by week, the children watched the workmen taking down the stones and stacking them in order. Week by week, the church walls became lower and lower, until at last the work was finished.

The workmen took away the last of the stones on a lorry, and nothing was left. Nothing was left except a big, bare patch of earth and the outline of the foundations.

The children felt sad because the church had gone, but in its place it left something they had never had before. It left an open space and some fresh air and a big patch of blue sky.

Then later, something wonderful happened. Little shoots of grass sprang up, and seeds blew in on the wind, and took root and began to grow. Soon the earth was green like a garden, and wild flowers were growing there.

"It's like a field," said Wendy.

"It makes a wonderful place to play," added Jean.

The children didn't know when the block of flats would be built, but meanwhile the ground became their playground. All the children from the street, and other children from other streets came to play there. They played with footballs and skipping ropes. They ran races and rolled on the grass. Someone brought an old plank and put it on a big stone they found in the loose earth. So they made a see-saw. The children were as happy as could be. Their parents were happy too because they knew the children had a safe place to play.

*   *   *   *   *   *

Meanwhile the stones of the old church had been loaded on to a cargo ship and taken across the sea to America. Then the stones had gone by train to a small town, where Mr Black lived. At last they had been unloaded on to a piece of land, and Mr Black soon had builders at work there.

They dug the foundations and started to build the walls. They put each stone in its right place, one on another, one on another.

*   *   *   *   *   *

In London the summer holidays came. The weather was warm and sunny, and the children played every day. They were so happy in their playground, that some of the little ones began to forget that there had ever been an old church there.

Then came some bad news.

"They're going to start building the block

of flats next month."

Everyone told everyone else, so that gloom hung over the grey streets like a great, black cloud.

"We'll lose our playground."

"We'll lose our beautiful field."

One morning a man drove up to the playground in a little van. It was one of the workmen who had helped to take the old church down. He could hardly believe what he saw! He had left bare earth and the outline of the foundations, but now there was a field of waving grass. There were yellow buttercups and dandelions. There were daisies and the lacy heads of cows' parsley.

"Hullo," said the workman. "You remember me, don't you?"

"Yes," replied the children, and they ran to talk to him. The workman walked over to the see-saw. Wendy was on one end. Jean was on the other end. Tom was standing in the middle.

"We've lost something," said the workman. "Mr Black phoned from America to say that a stone was missing from the church. It's a large stone with an angel's face carved on it, and it goes above the big East window. It may have fallen down inside and become buried long ago. Have any of you seen it?"

"No," replied the children.

"You haven't found any stones at all?"

"No," replied the children. The workman sighed.

"I didn't really think it would turn up," he said. "Oh well, don't let me stop your play."

One or two children went back to their games.

Tom gave a hard push on the see-saw with his foot. Wendy went up and Jean went down. The workman stood and gazed round. Then he asked,

"What's the see-saw resting on?"

"Just an old stone," replied Tom.

"Just an old stone!" cried the workman.

"Yes," said Tom. "It was half buried in the ground. Jimmy and I dug it out."

"Well!" said the workman. "Here am I, looking for an old stone, and there are you standing on one all the time. Jump down." Tom and Wendy and Jean jumped down. Tom and Jimmy lifted the plank out of the way.

"My word!" said the workman. "You've got a see-saw resting on an angel's face! I know it doesn't look much like a face. It's been worn by wind and rain over the years. But look—see the curve of the cheeks, and a bumpy bit where the stone curls used to be!"

He carried the stone to his van.

"I'll bring you something else to rest your

see-saw on. I promise."

He drove away and the children waved goodbye.

★　　★　　★　　★　　★　　★

It was several weeks before the workman came back. He brought a short log, and put the plank on it.

"Now you can use your see-saw again," he said. Then he added, "I've something to tell you." The children all came near. He waited till they were quiet and still. Then he said,

"Mr Black is a very kind man. I told you he used to live in these streets when he was a little boy. He knows what it's like to have nowhere to play. When he was told, in America, that you children had found the missing stone,

he wanted to give you a reward. So he paid a huge sum of money to the man who was going to build flats on this bit of land. Mr Black bought the land from him, so that it can be kept as a playground for you."

The workman thought the children would shout and cheer and jump for joy, but they didn't. They stood quite still and quite quiet.

A wind blew through the buttercups, and set the lacy heads of the cows' parsley shivering a little.

"A happy thought, isn't it?" said the workman. It was! It was such a happy thought that the children could find no words to say *how* happy.

Kandy the Kangaroo

When Kandy was very young, he didn't look like a kangaroo at all. He was a strange little thing without fur, but the most surprising thing about him was his size. His mother was more than a metre high, but Kandy was only two and a half centimetres! Perhaps you can hardly believe it, but it's quite true, for kangaroo babies are the most helpless of all animals. When Kandy was born, there seemed to be only one thing he could do. That was to climb, just once.

"Kandy," said his mother softly, "climb up through my fur, and you'll find a nice soft pouch waiting for you." So Kandy climbed slowly up and up through the long grey fur at the front of his mother's body—up and up and up. He climbed for half an hour, and then he came to the opening of her pouch. He slipped inside, and his mother gave him milk to drink. It was warm and cosy in the pouch, so there he stayed for weeks and weeks.

He didn't even peep at the world outside. So he knew nothing of the land of Australia, the mountains and the rocks, the long grass and the hot sun. He didn't see the place where his mother slept at night, nor the tall trees that gave her shade when the sun was hot in the daytime.

Kandy was so small that he saw nothing except the inside of his mother's pouch. But all the time he was there, lying snug and warm, he was changing and growing. Soft grey hair began to cover his tiny pink body. His ears began to stick up, and his nose grew more pointed, until soon he looked just like a baby kangaroo.

One warm, sunny day when Kandy was about four months old, he found he was big enough to see out of the top of his mother's pouch. So he put out his little furry face, and looked round with soft bright eyes.

"Mother, look at me," he said in a little whistling voice. His mother looked down at him, and made a noise that meant, "Oh, Kandy,

how nice to see you sitting up at last!" She felt
very proud of his pretty ears and his bright eyes,
and she took three big jumps across to where
eight other kangaroos were eating the grass.

"Look at my baby," she said.

The other kangaroos looked.

"I didn't even know you had a baby,"
remarked one. "He's been very quiet all this
time."

"What a lovely child he is," said the others.

Kandy's mother bent her head again, and ate
some more grass. Her teeth were long and sharp,
so that she could bite right down to the sweet
roots.

"That looks nice," thought Kandy. "I'd like to taste it." So he leaned out of the pouch a little further, and nibbled the fresh grass.

How exciting everything seemed to him. There was a blue sky and a hot sun, and different kinds of grass. There were big kangaroos like his mother, and a very big one indeed who was his grandfather, and there were two other babies who peeped out of their pouches and looked at him.

"Soon I'm going to jump out of my pouch, and hop about on the ground," he told them. But it looked a long way to jump so he decided not to do it that day after all. Besides there were all sorts of strange sights and sounds outside, and it was cosy and safe in his mother's pouch. He was sleepy too. Slowly Kandy tucked his head down into the pouch again, and closed his eyes.

"Tomorrow," he murmured. "I'll jump out of my pouch tomorrow." Then he fell asleep.

Next day he awoke early. He peeped out and

looked round. The morning was cool and calm, and the sun was just rising above the trees. His mother left her sleeping place, and stood up and stretched herself. The other kangaroos awoke too, and moved on together to a grassy patch. They moved with great jumps, swinging their long back legs forward between their front ones, and using their strong tails to help them.

"In a minute I'll jump out," thought Kandy. He waited till his mother was standing still beside a tuft of grass. Then he counted,

"One, two, three," and out he jumped.

Oh, what fun! He could hop, and jump, and sit back on his tail, or lean forward on his front legs. He could bite the grass right down to its sweet roots just as his mother did. His mother looked proudly at him, watching as he hopped a little distance away, tasting different pieces of grass.

"Oh this is fun!" said Kandy aloud. "I can hop and jump and nibble grass. I'm a grown-up kangaroo."

At that very moment the big grandfather kangaroo smelled danger. He thumped loudly on the ground with one of his back legs. The kangaroos looked up and stopped feeding. They all understood that signal. It meant, "Danger! Come close to me."

Only little Kandy did not understand. To him, it was just a loud noise that frightened him. He gave one big jump, the biggest he had ever given, and he landed head first in his mother's pouch.

"That's right," whispered his mother. "Stay here till the danger is over."

Kandy crouched down, and didn't even peep out, but he smelled a strange smell, and wondered what it was.

After a while his mother said,

"Grandfather says we may go on, for the danger is past."

"What was the strange smell?" asked Kandy.

"It was the smell of the wild dogs, the dingoes," she replied. "Always jump in my pouch when you smell that smell, Kandy."

Soon the sun became very hot, and the kangaroos went to a shady place among the trees, where they stretched out to rest in the shade.

When evening came, they moved to the river bank, where they ate some grass, and drank cool water. So the days passed, and Kandy hopped happily beside his mother. He followed her wherever she went, and jumped into her pouch whenever he was hungry or tired.

Late one afternoon Kandy and his mother wandered further away than usual from the other kangaroos. They went from one tuft of grass to another, without noticing how far they had gone. Suddenly a strange smell came over the air—the smell of dingoes. Like a flash, Kandy was in his mother's pouch. Like a statue stood his mother, only her nostrils moving a little, and her ears twitching. There in the deep shadows she stood, without a movement,

without a sound. She heard in the distance two dingoes hunting for their supper. She dared not move in case she sent the smell of kangaroo across the grass to them. So she stayed quite still, hoping and hoping that they would go a different way. But they did not. The smell of dingoes became stronger and stronger. Nearer came the dingoes, and nearer, like streaks of red fur in the setting sun.

The mother kangaroo knew that she must run, if she were to save Kandy and herself. With great leaps she bounded away, crashing through the bushes, startling the birds in the tree tops, frightening the tiny things in the

grass. The air was filled with hurrying footsteps and beating wings, with queer cries and the long, wild howl of the dingoes.

Kandy's heart beat fast. He had never travelled as swiftly as this. He was jogged and jolted in the pouch. One moment he was up, the next moment he was down. After a little while he peeped out of the pouch. He saw the dingoes close behind. They came closer and closer, until they were almost upon him.

In front was a water hole, and his mother was running straight towards it. There would be no escape now.

"Mother, Mother," panted Kandy. "Mind

the water."

But mother kangaroo knew what she was doing. Into the water hole she plunged, and as the two dingoes followed, she struck at them with her strong back legs, and scratched them with her long black claws. She caught hold of them and pushed them under the water, holding down their red faces until they choked and splashed and struggled to be free. At last the dingoes were too weary and hurt to fight any more, and they slunk away to their caves.

Then Kandy and his mother went back to their sleeping place. Mother lay down in the darkness, and Kandy curled up comfortably in her pouch. He was getting big now. He was seven months old. Soon he would be too big to use the pouch any more. One day he would be as big as his mother. He wondered if he would ever be as brave as she was. Kandy twitched his ears and closed his soft bright eyes. One day perhaps he would be as brave as his mother. One day.

The Story of Clocks

Long, long ago the only clock was the sun. People watched it rise above the hill, and knew that morning had come. They looked up when it was right overhead, and knew that the time was midday. They watched it sink lower and lower in the sky, and knew that evening was turning to night.

Shadows helped them too. They noticed that early in the morning, trees and people had long, thin shadows, but later they became short and fat, until at midday there were no shadows at all. In the afternoon the little fat shadows came again, and grew longer and thinner until the sun went down.

So someone (it might have been Lok or Shan) thought of a shadow clock. He stuck a stick in the ground, and scraped marks on the earth

where the shadow fell. He said, "When the shadow touches the first mark, I'll go and look for berries to eat, and I'll try to be back before the shadow touches the next mark."

For hundreds and hundreds of years after that, people still used shadow clocks, but very much better ones, called sundials. A sundial was carefully marked all the way round with small lines. It had a steel pointer fixed in the middle. The shadow of the pointer fell on one of the small lines, and moved slowly round to each one in turn.

There are many sundials even today, on the sides of old buildings, or resting on stone stands in gardens and parks.

People could tell the time then, by the sun in the daytime and the stars at night. But what were they to do on cold days when there was no sun, and on dark nights when clouds hid the stars? Different countries thought of different ways of telling the time.

In Egypt, water clocks were used. A water

clock was a pot or bowl with a tiny hole at the bottom. The water dripped through the hole, and ran into another pot which had lines inside. It always took the same time to empty the first pot, and fill the second.

In China there were lamp clocks. A lamp clock had a very long wick hanging down, with a knot and a space, a knot and a space, all the way. The flame at the end burnt up until it reached the first knot, then the second knot, and up gradually to the top.

In England in King Alfred's time there were candle clocks. A long candle was marked with lines about every two centimetres, and the flame burnt down to them one at a time.

In later years, hour glasses were used. An hour glass was like a large egg-timer. Sand dropped through from the top glass to the

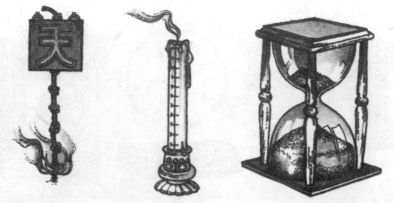

lower glass in one hour.

But as the years passed by, people began to need better clocks than these. At last someone found that a weight, swinging on a rod, always took the same time to swing from side to side. So the first pendulum clock was made.

After this, more and more clocks came into use. They were mostly ticking clocks with small wheels, worked by pendulums or springs. Many of the clocks in those days were very beautiful. Some of them had models of people or animals that came out of little doors and moved round every hour, or rang bells to tell the time.

Today we have many kinds of clocks. There are alarm clocks, cuckoo clocks, electric clocks and digital clocks, ticking away day and night, telling the hours, the minutes, the seconds.

Big Ben

Out across London booms the voice of Big Ben, striking the hours, the half hours and the quarter hours. The sound is carried by radio into homes all over the world, so that even children who have never been to Britain know something about Big Ben.

He is one of the best timekeepers there is for he is hardly ever more than a second wrong though once, a long while ago, he surprised everyone by striking twenty times at three o'clock in the morning.

Big Ben was built in Queen Victoria's time, and some people wanted him to be called Royal Victoria. Instead of this, he was named Big Ben after Sir Benjamin Hall, an important man in those days.

You know, of course, that Big Ben is very big, but do you know how big?

The clock tower is more than a hundred metres high, and it has three hundred and seventy-four steps inside. The hours are struck on a bell weighing thirteen and a half tonnes. The big hands, going round and round, travel more than a hundred-and-sixty kilometres a year.

The clock has four faces. Each one would just about cover the floor of your classroom. The figures are as tall perhaps as a six-month old baby. Your ruler would just fit in longways between the minute marks.

The hands are made of copper. If you stood upright on an adult's shoulders, you would be about the size of the small hands. If you put two beds together end to end, they would not be quite big enough to hold the big hands or the pendulum.

Perhaps you would like to take your ruler and measure the sizes for yourself. Do it on the ground, or along the side of a wall.

Here are the measurements:

The clock faces are almost seven metres across.

The pendulum is almost four metres long.

The figures are sixty centimetres high.

The minute lines are thirty-two centimetres apart.

The small hands are two hundred and seventy centimetres long.

The big hands are over four metres long.

No wonder he is called *Big* Ben!

What's the Time?

1. Make a shadow clock in your garden. Put a stick in the ground, and notice how long the shadow is at different times of the day.

2. Get an old tin, and make a tiny hole at the bottom. Then fill it with water, and you will have a water clock. See how long it takes to empty itself.

   You can make an hour glass in the same way. Fill a tin with fine sand instead of water.

3. Draw the different kinds of clocks that were used in the olden days. Write the name by each one.

4. Make a large circle on white paper. Write the hours carefully, and put in the small marks to show the minutes. Remember that there are five minutes between one figure and the next. There are sixty minutes altogether.

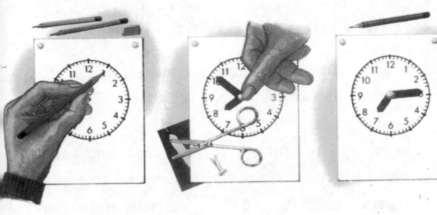

Draw and cut out the hands, and fix them to the middle of your clock, with a paper fastener or a pin. Turn the hands so that the time is quarter past seven.

5. Finish these sentences:
   a. I get up in the morning at ____.
   b. At ____ o'clock I have my breakfast.
   c. School starts at ____ o'clock.
   d. I come out of school at ____ o'clock.
   e. I have my dinner at ____ o'clock and my tea at ____ o'clock.
   f. I go to bed at ____ o'clock.
   g. I am in bed for ____ hours, and up for ____ hours.

The Dolphin Pilot

Once upon a time there was a dolphin playing around the shores of New Zealand. He swam lazily through the waves, splashing and rolling over, and jumping right out and back again just for fun. After a while he came to a place where the sea twisted and turned, and wound in among the mountains and the cliffs, almost like a river.

"I must explore this," he thought. So he swam between foam-splashed islands and jutting points of rock, into little bays and echoing sea caverns, and there he decided to make his home.

Now the stretch of water that he had chosen was called Pelorus Sound, but the dolphin cared nothing about its name. He knew only that it was cold and comfortable below, and sunny and spray-splashed above, and, most important of all, that there were plenty of cuttlefish, his favourite food. So he drifted into the shelter of a cave, where the salt water washed pleasantly over and around him, and there he rested.

He was a big dolphin, more than five metres in length, and except for his dark flippers, he was mostly white in colour, with touches of purple and blue.

He had not been long in his new home when, far away in the open sea, a steamer journeyed between the two main islands of New Zealand. Somehow, the dolphin knew that something strange was passing. Perhaps the ripples of the disturbed water came creeping into Pelorus Sound. Perhaps the noise of the engine came echoing and echoing into his cavern. Anyway, he didn't want to miss any fun.

"I simply must go and find out what it is," he murmured. He dashed through the water —past the mountains and the cliffs and the rocks—on and on till he came to the open sea.

"Ah!" he said. "A steamer. I expect it wants to go to the other island. I'll show it the

way." He darted to the front of the ship, and dived under it, first from one side, then from the other. He splashed playfully along with it, sometimes swimming ahead so fast that he looked like a streak of silver.

"This way, this way," he seemed to say, and

the people on the steamer crowded to the front of the ship and leaned over the rails eagerly to have a look at him.

"A white dolphin!" they cried. They watched him for a long time as he swam in front. Then as the ship drew nearer to the land, the dolphin darted away, and sped back to his home in Pelorus Sound.

A steamer travelled between the two main islands once every day and once every night. The dolphin soon learned when to expect it, and whenever he knew it was coming, he dashed out to meet it. He seemed to think that it was his job to lead it safely on its way. The sailors and the people on the ships began to look out for him.

"Here he comes!" they would cry, and because he swam from the direction of Pelorus Sound, they called him Pelorus Jack. People often travelled by steamer to see him. They would watch him swim and splash, and dive beneath the ship. They would shade their eyes from the sun and try to keep sight of him as he swam swiftly ahead.

"I wonder if he does it just for fun," they would say, "or because he really wants to guide the steamer?"

Whatever the reason, Pelorus Jack went on with his work. Even at night he would guide the steamer, travelling with it for a long time, dashing ahead in the darkness, a streak of white shining in the moonlight. Then he would swim back between the mountains and the cliffs, between the foam-splashed islands and jutting points of rock, into the little bays to his own echoing sea cavern.

Soon nearly everyone had heard of Pelorus Jack, the white dolphin that met the steamers day and night, and hardly ever missed.

The government of New Zealand sent out a notice saying that no one was to hurt him or any other dolphin of his kind. So Pelorus Jack was kept safe, and he lived to pilot the ships for over twenty years.

Cuttlefish

The cuttlefish is a strange-looking fish, rather like an octopus. When it is hungry, it hides in the sand and darts out on smaller fish or crabs, catching them with its long arms. It has ten arms.

Dolphins like to feed on cuttlefish. The cuttlefish is not big enough to fight them, but it has a clever way of escaping from them. It has a little bag of black powder, and when it is being chased, it lets the powder out into the water. The powder spreads like a cloud of black ink. This hides the cuttlefish, and gives it a chance to escape.

Battleships do the same kind of thing when they make smoke screens over the sea.

The ink of the cuttlefish is sometimes made into dark brown paint for us to use. Cuttlefish bones are often washed up on the sea-shore. They are flat, smooth and white. People who have canaries or budgies, sometimes push a cuttlefish bone between the bars of the cage. The birds use it to sharpen their beaks.

Next time you go to the sea, walk along the beach when the tide is out, and perhaps you will find a cuttlefish bone.

The Healing Waters

There was great sorrow among the American Indians, for with the snows of winter, a terrible sickness had come. In every family someone had fallen ill—a mother, a father or a child, and nothing seemed to make them well again.

Now there was one young Indian who knew that certain leaves and flowers could be used for medicine.

"If only I could find these healing plants," he thought, "I might save my people." He made up his mind to search until he found them, so he set off through the forest.

All day he looked for the healing plants, but the earth was white with snow, and not even a blade of grass could be seen. Soon he met a little rabbit.

"Tell me, rabbit," he said. "Where can I find the healing plants?" The rabbit knew that the plants wouldn't grow above the ground again until the snow melted and the spring came, and so he hurried away without answering.

Soon the Indian met a bear walking through the forest.

"Tell me, bear," he said. "Where can I find the healing plants?" The bear knew that the plants didn't grow in winter, so he too hurried away without answering.

For three days and nights the Indian wandered through the forest and over the hills, looking for the little plants from which he could make medicine to save his people. He spoke to all the animals he met on the way.

"Where can I find the healing plants?" he asked, but the animals knew that in winter he would never, never find them.

On the third night he was hungry and weak, and so tired that he fell down in the snow and slept. The animals and birds came to watch over him through the night. They remembered how kind he had always been to them. They were sorry for him, and wished they could help him.

As the Indian slept, he dreamed of a rippling stream. From the distance he heard the murmuring of its waters.

"Set us free," they seemed to say. "We are the healing waters. Set us free."

The Indian awoke, and saw that day had dawned. He thought of his dream, and it still seemed to him that he could hear the sound of the stream. He stood listening. It was not a dream now. He really could hear waters murmuring somewhere. He looked north and south and east and west.

He searched everywhere in the forest, but in vain. Then suddenly, he guessed that the waters must be underground. He scraped away the snow with the branch of a tree. He dug and he dug deep into the earth, until he was too weary and weak to dig any more. Then he saw something shining below—the waters of the buried stream!

Now that they were set free, they ran rippling through the trees, and down into the valley.

The Indian bathed his aching arms and legs in the healing stream, and in a moment he was well and strong.

"Oh!" he cried. "I've found the healing waters to save my people."

Quickly he made a pot of clay, and baked it hard in a fire of sticks. Then he dipped it into the stream, filled it up with the precious water, and hurried home again.

When he drew near the village, his friends ran out to meet him. Their faces were sad and weary, for the sickness was still in their homes. Eagerly they asked,

"Did you find the healing plants?"

"No," replied the Indian, "but I found the healing waters," and he told his friends where to go. So the people who were well hurried through the forest to the place where the stream splashed through the trees. They filled pots and jars, and carried them back to those who were ill. Gently they held the water to the lips of their children, and their mothers and fathers. They bathed their faces and their hands, and the sickness left them.

So everyone was made better, and the Indian who had found the hidden stream was given a new name, Chief of the Healing Waters, so that everyone might remember the precious gift he had brought.

The Voyage of Magnus Barefoot

King Magnus Barefoot stood upon the deck of his wooden ship, and gazed and gazed across the misty sea. A patch of pink seaweed drifted by, and a white sea-bird fluttered for a moment and then was gone.

"We must be near land," thought Magnus, "and if the wind hasn't blown us from our course, the land should be the west coast of Scotland."

Magnus was King of Norway in the days of long ago. He was strong, brave and handsome in his ruby-red tunic and his helmet of flashing gold. The handle of his sword was made of gold and ivory, and on his red shield was a picture of a golden lion.

It was early morning, and there was very little wind. Looking back at the great square sail of the ship, Magnus saw that it scarcely fluttered at all.

"Row!" he shouted. Down came the sail, and forty or fifty men ran to their places on the rowing seats. They put their swords and battle-axes beside them, hung their shields over the rails, and dipped their oars into the green-grey water. Magnus still gazed ahead, searching for land. Then out of the mist it rose like a mountain rising in a dream.

Soon the sun came out and the mist began to lift. Then Magnus saw rocky islands and the rugged coast of Scotland. He saw the green land of Kintyre, reaching out like an arm into the sea. He gazed at its wild beauty, and he said aloud, "I want this land for Norway."

In days of old, part of Scotland had belonged to Norway, but people seemed to have forgotten that. Part of it still belonged to Norway by right. Norway should have it back again from the Scots!

Magnus did not wish to make war, so he went to see Malcolm, King of Scotland, to ask him for Norway's share. Malcolm, King of Scotland, gave his answer.

"You may have all the land," he said, "round which you can take a ship."

All the land round which you can take a ship! That meant all the land with sea round it—all the islands—the Orkneys, the Shetlands and the Hebrides. But it did not mean the green land of Kintyre reaching out like an arm into the sea, and it was Kintyre that Magnus wanted most of all.

He went back to his ship, with its curved front and its great square sail. He sailed round the rocky islands, and, when the wind didn't blow the right way, his men rowed, dipping their oars in and out of the green-grey water. Round the large islands went Magnus, and round the small islands, round the Orkneys, the Shetlands and the Hebrides. At last all the islands on the west coast of Scotland were his, for Norway; but still he wanted the land of Kintyre.

Again he sailed in his ship and gazed at Kintyre, watching the sea wash round it on all sides but one. All sides but one! That gave him an idea. He called his men to him, and told them of his plan. Some of them laughed. Some thought he was greedy. Some thought he was clever, but they all agreed to help him.

They rowed the ship to the place where Kintyre stretched out from the mainland. Round its rocky coast they rowed, right round until they came to the side where there was land instead of sea. Then the men jumped out, fastened ropes to the ship, and pulled it up on the beach.

Only Magnus Barefoot, King of Norway, stayed in the ship. Proudly he stood in his ruby-red tunic and his helmet of flashing gold. In one hand he held his sword, with its handle of gold and ivory. In the other hand he held his red shield, with its golden lion shining in the sun.

"Ready!" he called.

His men gave a great pull. Slowly the wooden ship moved. It creaked and scraped, and its big square sail fluttered in the wind. With all their strength the men pulled at the ropes, dragging the ship across the strip of land, until they reached the sea on the other side.

Down into the green-grey water went the ship again. Magnus laughed, for he had truly taken a ship all round the land of Kintyre. So Kintyre belonged to Norway.

Fairy Rings

If you get up very early, when the grass is wet with dew, you may be lucky enough to see a fairy ring. There it will be—a ring of small white toadstools, looking up to the sunshine in a perfect circle. You will know that the toadstools have grown suddenly, silently, during the night. But how did they come to be in such a beautiful ring?

That is a question which has puzzled country people all through the ages. They used to think the fairies danced in the moonlight, and left their tiny footprints; and the toadstools grew up in the footprints, marking the ring where the fairies had danced.

For hundreds and hundreds of years people believed this. Then at last, they began to have other ideas. Some said the fairy rings were made by ants. Some said they were made by the wind. Some said they were made by thunder or lightning, but no one knew for certain.

Why *do* toadstools sometimes grow in a perfect circle? How *do* fairy rings come?

Here is the real answer.

Most plants have flowers that make seeds. But the toadstool has no flowers; and instead of seeds, it drops tiny specks of itself, called spores. The spores fall to the ground in a little ring round the toadstool. The toadstool fades, and later the spores grow into new toadstools. They make the first fairy ring, but a very small one.

Then those toadstools drop spores all round themselves, and fade too. Now the earth on the inside of the ring has had its goodness used up by those toadstools, so the spores that fall there never grow. But the spores that fall on

125

the good earth outside the ring find all they
need to make them grow, and once more a ring
of toadstools appears in the night. This time it
is a bigger ring.

The same thing happens again. The new
toadstools drop spores, and fade. The spores
that fall on the inside of the ring do not grow,
because the goodness has been taken from the
earth by the other toadstools. But the spores
that fall on the good earth outside the ring *do*
grow.

So the ring becomes wider and wider, as
old toadstools die, and new ones grow. The
white toadstools stand in a perfect circle,
looking up to the sunshine, and people who
are out early in the morning smile and say,

"Oh, look! A fairy ring!"

Nana Miriam
and the Monster

Many years ago, by the banks of the River Niger in Africa, there lived a young woman called Nana Miriam.

The men of her tribe were hunters, farmers and fishermen. As they grew up, the boys of the tribe were taught these skills. Nana's father had no son, and so he taught her all he knew.

By the time she grew to be a young woman Nana Miriam was as brave and clever as any man of the tribe, and as strong too. Indeed she was stronger than many. Her father had taught her well. She knew all there was to know about the beasts of the forests and rivers. She knew when the corn would ripen and where the largest fish were to be caught.

The people of the tribe were proud of Nana Miriam. They called her the Little Warrior, and spoke of her great skills.

But Nana Miriam had a secret. She had one

skill that none of her people knew about. When she was very small her father had discovered that she had a special power, and he had taught her many magic spells. Nana Miriam kept her gift a secret until the day came when her tribe needed it.

It happened like this.

By the banks of the great River Niger lived a terrible monster. At times it took the shape of a huge hippopotamus, breathing out fire. At other times it looked more like a lion, then a snake. This evil monster was able to change its shape as it wished.

For many years it lived by the river. It ate the corn that the women grew in their fields. It drove away the animals so that the hunters could find no meat for their children. The people became poor and hungry.

Many men tried to kill the monster but none of them succeeded.

Nana Miriam's father was one of those who tried. He took his best and sharpest hunting spears and tracked the monster for many days and nights. He came upon it at last on a muddy bank by the river. He crept up and threw his spears, but the monster heard him coming and turned into a great ball of fire, so that the spears were burned to ashes.

Other men tried to kill the monster. Some even came from other tribes along the river. But one by one they were all driven back.

Still the monster went on eating the corn and hunting the animals so that the people often had to go without food, and their children cried because they were hungry.

Nana Miriam listened to the stories the hunters told.

"Is there no one who can kill this monster?" she asked her father.

"No one," he said, shaking his head sadly.

"Then I'll do it myself," said Nana Miriam. Her father and the people of the village were afraid. They tried to stop her, but she shook her head.

"I will go," she said. "And I won't return until I have killed this monster and set my people free."

"Then take our spears, Nana Miriam," said the warriors of the tribe, "for you have none of your own."

Nana Miriam shook her head. She took with her only a small bag of powder, and she set out to find the monster.

She came upon it in a cornfield by the river bank. Its huge teeth were tearing and crunching at the little plants. As soon as it heard Nana Miriam it stopped and lifted its ugly hippo-

potamus head. It knew she had come to attack
it, and it laughed so much that it nearly choked
itself on a mouthful of corn.

"Laugh as much as you like!" said Nana
Miriam. "It'll be for the last time!"

At that the monster became angry. It roared
a fearful roar, and its breath set fire to the
earth.

A huge wall of fire flamed up all around it,
but Nana Miriam was ready for that. She pulled
open her bag and scattered some of the powder.
Instantly the flames turned to water and the
monster stood in a huge puddle of mud.

Then it spun round and round, tossing its head. The mud turned to dust, and the dust became a wall of iron.

Nana Miriam said not a word. She too spun round, and in her hand there appeared a magic hammer. She swung it above her head and with one ringing blow she struck the wall of iron. It shattered into a thousand pieces, leaving the monster shaking its head in amazement at

the noise! It was beginning to understand that Nana Miriam's magic was too strong for it.

"The time has come for me to leave," said the monster to itself and it turned itself into a stream of water that trickled across the field into the great River Niger.

But quick as a flash Nana Miriam chanted a spell. Three times she spun round and then she threw the rest of her powder into the river.

At once the mighty Niger was turned into a tiny stream and the monster was left in the sticky mud.

"Come out and fight," shouted Nana Miriam. "What are you doing, playing in the mud like a child?"

The monster roared and raged until the forests echoed with its terrible voice, and the birds flew off in fear.

Nana Miriam's father heard the noise and hurried to the riverbank to see what had happened.

"Nana Miriam," he shouted. "Nana Miriam, are you all right?"

The monster heard him. It lowered its terrible head and charged towards him. Its huge feet thundered across the earth, shaking the great forest trees until the monkeys fled in fear.

"Stop, Father!" shouted Nana Miriam. "Stay where you are!"

He stood perfectly still as the monster

charged towards him. And then just as it seemed
as if its fiery breath would surely burn him to
a cinder, Nana Miriam jumped from behind a
bush.

She seized the monster by its back leg, and
with all her strength and magic she swung it
round and round her head.

Then with one huge effort she hurled the

monster across the mighty River Niger and it fell dead on the stones of the other bank. The mountains rang with the sound of the crash. The cheers and cries of delight from Nana Miriam and her father rang with it.

From that day the people of Nana Miriam's tribe lived in peace and happiness, with plenty of food for all.

The story of Nana Miriam's brave fight soon spread. It was told in songs and stories everywhere along the banks of the great River Niger, and it is told to this day.

The Story of Writing

No one knows when writing began. Perhaps a cave girl sat on the sand, and made wavy lines in it with her finger. Perhaps a cave boy sat by the river, picked up a stick, and drew animals in the wet clay. Perhaps a cave man went out hunting, and before he went he took a sharp stone, and scraped a picture of a bear on the wall of his cave.

When his family came in, they saw it and said;

"He must have gone to hunt a bear."

That may have been how the first letter in the world was written. No one knows. But we do know that the earliest writing was picture writing.

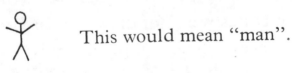 This would mean "man".

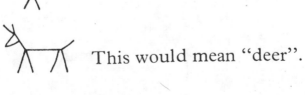 This would mean "deer".

This would mean "tree".

 This would mean "sun", or "day".

So, someone who wished to leave a message saying,

"I caught a deer by the tree today," would leave this picture message drawn on clay, or cut on a rock:

 The person who found it might not guess the exact words, but he would understand what was meant.

Soon, when people began to write more, the pictures were not drawn so carefully. They may have changed a little, like this:

man

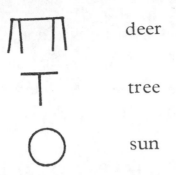

deer

tree

sun

After a while, they were no longer pictures, but signs, as the letters and sounds we use today are signs. Sometimes the clay on which they were written was baked hard in the sun, and kept for a long time. Sometimes the writing was scratched on big leaves, or on tablets of stone.

Then a kind of picture writing was made, where the drawings meant the sound of the words as they were spoken, instead of the things in the pictures.

The picture of a bee, perhaps, no longer meant a bee, but the sound zzzzz.

This sort of writing led to the making of the alphabet, a, b, c, which spread quickly from one country to another.

For a long while, writing was done on leaves of plants, joined together in strips, or on linen or skins of animals. A reed or a feather was cut to a point and used as a pen. Ink was made from cuttlefish.

People wrote now, not only to give messages to their friends, but because they wanted to write. They liked to write about the things they saw around them. They liked to write down their thoughts, their songs and their stories. So, books began—books in long pieces, that rolled up, and were tied with grass or thread. There was only one of each book, unless the writer made another, by carefully copying it out, word for word. This of course took a very long time, so only rich people could afford to buy books.

Paper was first made by the Chinese, but its secret was not learned by other countries until many hundreds of years later. Paper can be made from plants, rags or wood.

The most important thing in the story of

writing was the making of the printing press
in Holland and Germany. The first man to set
up a printing press in England was William
Caxton. What a difference this made to people!
A printing press could make hundreds of copies
of a book instead of just one.

Very soon more printing presses were made,
and more books were sold. Now many people
wanted to read, and books became cheap, so
that even poor people could buy them. Children
who had never been out of their own little

village could learn from books about lands far away. And instead of waiting for someone to tell them stories, they could learn to read stories for themselves.

The paper was no longer rolled. It was folded, and stitched between covers, like the books we know. Some books were plain, and cost little, but others had covers of silk or leather, purple velvet, or carved ivory, with little locks of gold or wonderful patterns of precious jewels.

Today we have papers and pencils and pens. We have newspapers and story books—hundreds and hundreds of story books to make us happy.

What a lot of things have happened since the little cave girl made wavy lines on the sand with her finger, and the little cave boy drew animal pictures in the clay. They didn't know, did they, that they were writing the very first books?

Fun with Writing

1. Roll a piece of plasticine, and press it out, so that it is as large and flat as possible. Use a matchstick, and write some messages in picture writing.
2. Try to scratch a message on a flat piece of stone, using a pin or a nail.
3. Copy these pictures on paper. Write beside each one the word you think it means:

4. Pretend we use picture writing today. Make some pictures, and write their names.
5. Copy a poem on a piece of paper. Do it in your best writing, and draw a pattern round the edge. Roll the paper into a thin roll like a book of long ago. Tie it with ribbon or cotton.
6. Now make another book, by folding and cutting paper. Fix the pages together with

string or staples. Make the cover as beautiful as possible. Colour it. Give the book a name, and write a story inside.

7. Here is a letter, partly in ordinary writing, and partly in picture writing. See if you can write it, putting in words where the pictures come: -

Dear John,

A  gave me a . It likes to eat. I am making a for it. I shall stand the under the beside the

Love from
Michael.